Please return/renew this item by the
last date shown to avoid a charge.
Books may also be renewed by phone
and Internet. May not be renewed if
required by another reader.
www.libraries.barnet.gov.uk

LONDON BOROUGH

'Trouble Undercover'
An original concept by Katie Dale
© Katie Dale

Illustrated by Kaley McCabe

Published by MAVERICK ARTS PUBLISHING LTD
Studio 11, City Business Centre, 6 Brighton Road,
Horsham, West Sussex, RH13 5BB
© Maverick Arts Publishing Limited August 2021
+44 (0)1403 256941

A CIP catalogue record for this book is available at the British Library.

ISBN 978-1-84886-803-8

www.maverickbooks.co.uk

This book is rated as: Brown Band (Guided Reading)

Trouble
Undercover

Written by
Katie Dale

Illustrated by
Kaley McCabe

Chapter 1

CLATTER! A large gold envelope fell through Dev's letterbox. It made such a loud noise that he looked up from his crossword puzzle. Dev was an *expert* at puzzles of all kinds, and usually nothing could distract him until he finished. But this envelope was very strange. It was gold, marked 'TOP SECRET' and addressed to Dev! Could it be the results of the coding contest he'd entered last month?

Dev opened it quickly. Inside was a typed letter and a gold card with fancy writing:

Solve this coded message to earn your place—

tell no one but your mum.

Dev grinned. Another puzzle! He read the coded message eagerly:

Congratulations! Come on! Try winning all the colour coding monkey contest competitions! This time! is now your moment? invitation attached to come join in the Monkey Mysteriosa Party! Academy, for the silly! secret party! boarding airplanes! school not for you! spies! in The jungle bus soon will depart! collect bananas you monkey and tell your silly mum nothing! from Montgomery your friend. house party on every Tuesday! always at night 5 hundred o'clock! Still in costumes the next morning. Don't Remember— just tell me! no worries! one opportunity—but forget your silly mum! Jungle Spies rule! who cares? cannot everyone be invited! trusted Monkeys will never not ever be not permitted.

Dev frowned. It was a code he'd never seen before... what could it mean? It couldn't *really* be about monkeys, could it?

Suddenly he cracked it! He crossed out every other word, and the true message was revealed:

Congratulations on winning the coding contest! This is your invitation to join the Mysteriosa Academy, the secret boarding school for spies! The bus will collect you and your mum from your house on Tuesday at 5 o'clock in the morning. Remember—tell no one but your mum! Spies who cannot be trusted will not be permitted.

Excitement fizzed through Dev like electricity. He was going to spy school!

Chapter 2

Dev was even more excited early on Tuesday morning when a gold electric-powered bus pulled up outside his house!

"Mum!" he called. "Time to go!"

"Are you sure you want to go to a boarding school?" his mum asked.

"It's not too late to change your mind!"

Dev bit his lip.

"I'll miss you, Mum," he said. "But this is my chance to be a real spy! I can't miss it!"

His mum beamed. "Then we'd better not miss the bus! Come on!"

They hurried outside.

The bus was already quite full of children and their parents. Dev looked around for a free seat.

"Come and sit with us!" a girl called from the back row. Dev and his mum hurried over.

"I'm Anya," the girl said. "And this is Clare and Mo. We're *so* excited! Are you?"

Dev beamed and nodded. "I can't wait to be a spy!"

"I wonder where the academy is?" Clare said. "There was no address on the invitation."

"The location is secret!" the driver called out, handing out blindfolds. "In order to keep it that way, please wear your blindfold for the rest of the journey."

It was odd wearing a blindfold. Dev was *so* tempted to have a tiny peek. Surely no one would know? Suddenly the bus stopped. Had they reached the academy already?

"Clare!" the driver snapped. "You peeked from your blindfold. Please leave the bus."

"But..." Clare protested. "It was only for a second..."

"Leave," he repeated. "Spies who cannot be trusted are not permitted."

Clare and her dad left sadly.

Dev gulped. He was glad he hadn't peeked!

Finally the bus stopped again. Had someone else peeked?

"Now you may remove your blindfolds," the driver said.

Dev pulled his blindfold off and gasped. They were outside an incredible futuristic windowless building!

"Welcome to the Mysteriosa Academy!" the driver beamed.

Chapter 3

Once all the parents had returned home, Dev and the other trainees soon settled in. Dev loved his new school. Everything was so different! Instead of history and maths, they learned coding and camouflage!

Instead of science and sports, they learned gadgets and stealth! Mo and Anya soon became Dev's best friends and they had never had so much fun!

But then one day, they were called into the headmaster's office. Dev gulped. He hoped he hadn't accidentally broken a school rule. He'd hate to leave the Mysteriosa Academy already!

But to his surprise, the headmaster smiled at them all. "It is time for your first mission!"

Dev's eyes widened. How exciting!

"You'll be going undercover," the headmaster explained, handing Mo a spacesuit, Dev a pirate outfit, and Anya a sparkly pink fairy dress. Anya grimaced. She hated pink, and never wore dresses!

This was the strangest camouflage Dev had ever seen—were they on a mission to Mars, a pirate ship or a fairy kingdom?!

"You will be going to a fancy dress birthday party," the headmaster explained. "An evil millionaire has invited her daughter's whole school to the party, so you should be able to get in without suspicion."

"An evil millionaire?" Mo gulped.

"Indeed," the headmaster nodded. "She stole the princess's priceless diamond tiara from the palace. Your mission is to retrieve it."

Dev's stomach fluttered with excitement.

"You'll each have a gadget to help you on your mission," the headmaster continued, opening a box. Dev's eyes lit up. He loved gadgets!

"Anya, this wand will block all electricity to anything it touches. Mo, your space helmet has super-hearing, and Dev, your pirate eye-patch lets you see through walls."

"Cool!" Dev cried, trying it out. He looked straight through the wall and saw the secretary secretly picking her nose. He stifled a giggle.

"This is no laughing matter," the headmaster said. "The princess herself is counting on you. Make me proud."

"We will!" Dev, Anya and Mo said, beaming.

Chapter 4

Finally the day of the party arrived. Nerves fluttered in Dev's stomach as they approached the queue outside the mansion.

"Welcome to my party!" a little blonde girl standing at the door squealed.

"That must be Lottie—the evil millionaire's daughter," Dev whispered.

"And that must be the evil millionaire," Anya pointed at a tall blonde lady standing next to Lottie.

"What if Lottie sees us and knows we don't go to her school?" Mo said, panicking.

"*You're* okay, she can't see your face!" Anya hissed.

Dev gulped. He crossed his fingers as they reached the front door.

Lottie looked at Dev, then Anya, then frowned. Oh no! Was their mission over before it had even begun?!

Suddenly Lottie laughed. "These costumes are amazing! I don't even recognise half the kids here! Welcome to my party!"

Dev and Anya smiled at each other, relieved.

But their relief didn't last long. The house was enormous. How would they ever find the tiara?

"If you were an evil millionaire, where would you hide a diamond tiara?" Mo asked Anya.

"Why are you asking me? Because I'm a girl?" Anya scowled. "Like I know anything about jewellery! I still don't know why I had to wear a stupid dress!"

"Well, if Dev or I had worn it people would have been suspicious!" Mo grinned.

"Shh," Dev hissed as Lottie looked over at them. "We're making people suspicious right now! Let's find the tiara and get out of here."

Together, they carefully searched the house. Mo listened out for people coming and Dev kept watch as Anya searched each room... until they reached a door that was locked.

"Rats!" Anya hissed, rattling the handle.

"Maybe the tiara's not in there anyway?" Mo said hopefully.

Dev used his eye-patch to look through the wall.

Inside was a beautiful bedroom with a four-poster bed, a dressing table filled with perfume and make-up, a sofa... and a safe.

Dev sighed. "If I was an evil millionaire, that's where I'd keep a stolen tiara."

"But how will we get in?" Anya sighed.

"Can't you pick the lock with a hairpin?" Mo said.

"I haven't got a hairpin," Anya scowled. "Besides the lock's electric!"

"That's it!" Dev said. "Use your magic wand!"

"Of course!" Anya said, tapping the lock with her wand. The door opened and they hurried inside.

"Use your wand on the safe, Anya!" Dev hissed.

"On it!" Anya grinned. She tapped the safe and the door opened, revealing a sparkling diamond tiara.

Dev laughed. "That was almost too easy!"

"Wait—I can hear someone coming!" Mo hissed, shutting the safe. "Quick—hide!"

Dev hid behind the bed, just as the bedroom door swung open. Lottie's mum walked in, marched straight to the safe, and grabbed the tiara! Oh no!

Worse still, as she walked back towards the door, she stopped and spotted Anya's pink sash sticking out from behind the sofa...

"What are you doing in here, little girl?" she demanded.

Dev gulped. The evil millionaire had caught Anya!

Chapter 5

"Um…" Anya hesitated. "I'm playing hide-and-seek! You found me! Congratulations!"

The evil millionaire looked confused.

"What a pretty dress!" Anya said quickly. "You're a princess like me! You even have a beautiful tiara!"

The evil millionaire smiled. "Thank you," she said, putting the tiara on her head. "My daughter insisted I wore it. Come on, let's go back to the party."

The evil millionaire swept out of the room, taking Anya with her.

"What do we do now?" hissed Mo. "How will we get the tiara now she's wearing it?"

Dev sighed. "We have to try."

They hurried downstairs to find Lottie making Anya curtsey.

"Let's all play princesses!" Lottie squealed.

"Poor Anya," Dev sighed, looking at her pained expression. "This is her worst nightmare!"

"It's about to get worse," Mo gasped, pointing at Lottie—who had just grabbed Anya's wand!

"Give that back!" Anya cried, reaching for the wand.

"No! It's my party and I want to play with it!" Lottie squealed. As she backed away the wand knocked the stereo and instantly the music stopped.

Lottie frowned. She tapped the stereo again. As the music came back on her eyes lit up. "It's magic!"

"Uh-oh," Dev said, panicking. "We have to get that wand back—quick!"

But suddenly the room was plunged into darkness.

"Happy birthday to you..." sang the millionaire, as she walked in holding a cake lit with candles. Everyone quickly joined in. "Happy birthday to you..."

"This is my chance," Mo hissed, creeping up behind the millionaire.

"Happy birthday, dear Lottie..." Dev sang, watching anxiously as Mo reached for the tiara...

"Happy birthday to—AARGH!" The millionaire shrieked as Mo grabbed her tiara. She dropped the cake, the candles went out, and the room was pitch black once more.

"Quick—let's get out of here!" Anya cried.

Dev stumbled across the room, searching desperately for the exit... when suddenly all the lights flicked back on.

Chapter 6

"My tiara!" Lottie's mum cried, looking around anxiously. "Who took it?"

Dev glanced nervously at Mo, but he wasn't holding the tiara. Dev couldn't see it anywhere.

Lottie's mum took a deep breath, and forced a smile. "Now children, I'm not cross, I just want my tiara back, okay? Whoever took it, bring it to me now."

No one moved. Lottie's mum's smile disappeared.

"Okay, everyone line up against the wall. Time to play Find the Fibber!"

One by one, Lottie's mum searched each child. Dev watched anxiously as she searched Mo...

But she moved straight on! Phew! Mo flashed Dev a thumbs-up and hurried out of the room.

"We've got to get out of here!" Dev hissed to Anya after they'd been searched.

"Not without my wand!" Anya said, grabbing it from Lottie.

"Pleeeease let me keep it!" Lottie begged. "It's the

best birthday present I've got!"

"Seriously?" Anya scoffed, pointing at Lottie's huge pile of presents. "But you've got a computer, a puppy and an electric scooter!"

"Come on, we've got to go!" Dev hissed urgently, grabbing Anya's arm and hurrying to the door.

Suddenly Lottie's mum burst into tears. "Where can my tiara be?!" she wailed. "I can't lose it! It's one of my only mementoes of my wedding day!"

Dev stopped running and frowned. "When was your wedding?"

"Ten years ago," Lottie's mum sniffed, pointing to a large wedding photograph on the window-ledge.

"Nearly everything else from that day got destroyed in a fire, but luckily I kept my tiara in my safe."

Dev and Anya stared at the wedding photograph and gasped. It was definitely the same tiara... so how could it be the princess's?

"If that's really Lottie's mum's tiara..." Anya whispered, turning pale. "Then we're the thieves, not her!"

"We have to stop Mo!" Dev cried.

"Where is he?" Anya cried, looking around. "Use your eye-patch, Dev!"

Dev spotted Mo racing down the garden.

"He's already halfway to the pick-up point!" Dev wailed. "We'll never catch him in time!"

"Oh yes we will," said Anya, grabbing Lottie's electric scooter. They jumped on, and zoomed out through the patio doors.

"Stop, thieves!" Lottie screamed. Two security guards appeared from nowhere and gave chase.

"Faster, Anya!" Dev cried. They had to catch Mo— and not be caught themselves!

Chapter 7

Anya and Dev zoomed through the garden, narrowly avoiding statues, ponds and plant pots.

"Mo, stop!" Anya yelled, spotting him on top of the fence.

"I've got the princess's tiara!" Mo called happily.

"It's not the princess's," Dev explained as they stopped at the fence. "It's Lottie's mum's—she wore it at her wedding ten years ago!"

"That's impossible!" he said. "She must be lying!"

"There's a photo," Anya said. "We've been tricked into stealing it!"

Mo hesitated. "But... why would the headmaster trick us?"

"Maybe he's a thief," Dev said, turning pale.

"Get a move on!" came a gruff voice.

Dev used his eye-patch to look into the waiting getaway car. The driver held a mobile phone to his ear as he glared up at Mo.

"Have you got the tiara or not?" he yelled.

Mo glanced from Anya and Dev to the driver, looking as if he couldn't make up his mind. Then suddenly he snatched Anya's wand, and ran towards the getaway car!

"No!" Anya and Dev yelled as Mo disappeared from sight—just as Lottie's security guards caught up with them.

"He took the tiara!" Anya sighed, pointing to Mo. "You're too late."

Mo jumped into the electric getaway car.

Dev used his eye-patch to look inside.

"You made the right choice," the driver said, smiling at Mo and revving the engine.

"I did," Mo said, tapping the car with Anya's wand. Instantly, the engine cut out. "Whoops!" he laughed.

Dev sighed with relief—Mo wasn't running away after all!

"Eh?" the driver gasped, turning purple as he glared angrily at Mo. "What have you done?"

Mo gulped. Just then, the two security guards jumped over the fence. The getaway driver turned pale, jumped out of the car, and fled.

"Quick! He's getting away!" Mo yelled, pointing.

The security guards soon caught up with the driver, just as Anya and Dev climbed over the fence—followed by Lottie's mum.

"There's no sign of the tiara," the security guards sighed.

"That's because it's here!" Mo grinned, taking off his helmet. He was wearing it!

"Suits you!" Anya giggled. "You look like a fairy princess spaceman—especially with my wand!"

Mo curtseyed and everyone laughed.

"But... why did you take it?" Lottie's mum asked. "What on earth is going on?"

Dev and Anya told her all about the spy school.

"Our headmaster told us to retrieve the stolen tiara—but now we think he wanted us to steal it instead!" Dev explained.

Anya nodded. "We thought he'd got away with it when you got into the getaway car, Mo!"

"I wasn't sure what to believe," Mo confessed, "But then my helmet's super-hearing overheard the headmaster speaking to the driver on the phone.

He told him to hurry up because he had a buyer ready to pay a fortune for the tiara, so I knew he wasn't going to return it to the princess! So I zapped the electric car with Anya's wand and the getaway car couldn't get away!"

"Brilliant!" Anya beamed.

"Phew!" Lottie's mum smiled.

"The police are on their way to arrest the driver," her security guard said.

"But what about the headmaster?" Anya said, "He's the real villain, but how will we find him? We don't even know where the school is!"

Everyone sighed. Then Dev grinned. He picked up the Sat Nav from the car and scrolled to 'Last Destination'.

"Now we do!" he beamed.

"Hurray!" everyone cheered.

Chapter 8

The headmaster was arrested, and the Mysteriosa Academy was closed down. Dev was happy to return home to his mum, and thrilled to have defeated a criminal mastermind, but he couldn't help feeling a bit sad that he was no longer going to spy school—and he missed Anya and Mo terribly.

Then one day...

CLATTER! A silver envelope fell through his letterbox. Dev held his breath as he opened it. It was another coded message!

Efbs Efw, zpv boe zpvs npuifs bsf jowjufe up uif

qbmbdf po uif gpvsui pg Bqsjm bu uxp q.n.

Dev sighed, and dropped it in the bin—he wasn't

going to be tricked again!

But, five minutes later, he took the paper out of

the bin again. Dev couldn't resist a puzzle!

Dev stared at the message, then grinned. "Each

letter stands for the one before it!" Quickly, he

deciphered the message and showed his mum.

Dear Dev, you and your mother are invited to the

palace on the fourth of April at two p.m.

Dev frowned. "Could it be another trick?"

His mum raised an eyebrow. "There's only one way

to find out!"

When they got to the palace, Dev was surprised to

see Anya and Mo waiting outside too!

"What do you think this is about?" Dev asked anxiously.

"Maybe we're getting a medal!" Anya said excitedly.

"Or a huge reward!" Mo suggested. "Maybe we'll be allowed to pick what we get! I'd choose a year's supply of chocolate! No, that's silly—a *lifetime's* supply of chocolate!"

Anya and Dev laughed.

Suddenly the gates opened.

"Come in," said a man in a smart suit and very shiny shoes. Dev gulped.

The man led them into the palace, and down a long corridor to a room with no windows.

"Thank you for all you did to shut down the fake spy school," he said, closing the door behind them.

"Mr Mysteriosa had been using children to steal all sorts of valuables for years. We're very grateful that you helped stop him."

Dev smiled.

"Is there a reward?" Mo asked hopefully.

"Of sorts," the man smiled. "We would like to invite you to join a *real* spy school."

Excitement fizzed through Dev's veins. This was the best reward he could have hoped for! But then he frowned. "How do we know this isn't another fake

spy school?" he said.

"Yes," Anya frowned. "How can we be sure we'll be working for the good guys this time?"

"Because this time you'll be working for me," said a voice behind them.

Anya, Dev and Mo whirled round to see... the princess!

Dev beamed at Anya and Mo, who grinned back. You couldn't be surer than that! It seemed their spying days weren't over yet after all!

Discussion Points

1. How did Dev earn a place at the Mysteriosa Academy?

2. What did Anya's gadget wand do?

a) Helps her see through walls

b) Blocks any electricity it touches

c) Lets her listen to people talk from far away

3. What was your favourite part of the story?

4. Who was the real thief in the end?

5. Why do you think Mo initially didn't believe Anya and Dev about the tiara?

6. Who was your favourite character and why?

7. There were moments in the story when Dev had to **think outside the box**. Where do you think the story shows this most?

8. What do you think happens after the end of the story?

Book Bands for Guided Reading

The Institute of Education book banding system is a scale of colours that reflects the various levels of reading difficulty. The bands are assigned by taking into account the content, the language style, the layout and phonics. Word, phrase and sentence level work is also taken into consideration.

The Maverick Readers Scheme is a bright, attractive range of books covering the pink to grey bands. All of these books have been book banded for guided reading to the industry standard and edited by a leading educational consultant.

Pink
Red
Yellow
Blue
Green
Orange
Turquoise
Purple
Gold
White
Lime
Brown
Grey

To view the whole Maverick Readers scheme, visit our website at

www.maverickearlyreaders.com

Or scan the QR code to view our scheme instantly!

Maverick Chapter Readers
(From Lime to Grey Band)